Curious Michael and His Mysterious Baby Sister

Written by

Mosina Jordan

Illustrated by Valerie Bouthyette

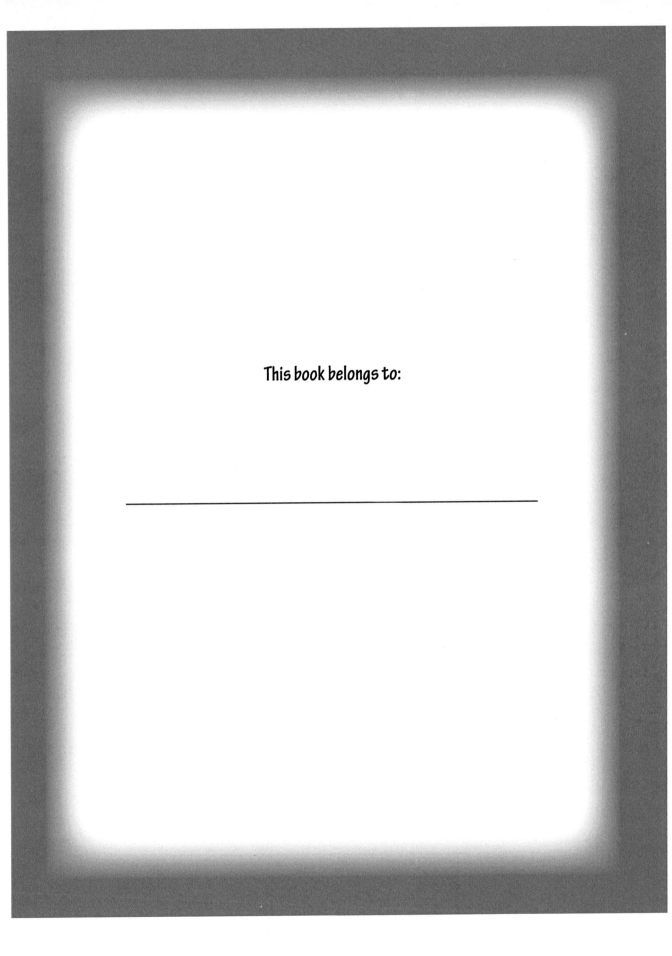

This book belongs to:

_____

Michael lived in an apartment in the city
with his mother and father, and five-month old sister.

Michael was eighteen months old and just becoming aware
of the world around him - exploring,
wondering why and climbing in and out of things.

Michael and his baby sister shared a room.
They played there during the day, and at night
the baby slept in a crib in one corner of the room
and Michael slept in his bed in another corner.

Every night, when she was put into her crib,
the baby would cry and cry.

Michael would lie in bed listening to the
baby cry. He tried very hard to fall asleep,
but he just couldn't.

The baby was making too much noise.

Michael didn't understand why the baby always cried when she was put into her crib.

It hadn't been too long ago that Michael had done the very same thing, but he had forgotten all about that.

Michael's mommy came into the room to take the baby out.

A few moments later she returned carrying the baby asleep in her arms.

Michael wondered what could have happened to make the baby go to sleep so quickly. She had been screaming only a moment ago. Michael thought, "When the baby cries again, I'll go see what happens to her.

The next night, the baby cried as usual, screaming at the top of her lungs. Mommy came in and took the baby out of the room.

As soon as Mommy and the baby disappeared, Michael hopped out of bed and walked to the door. Suddenly he heard his mother say, "Michael, get back into bed!"

Her strong voice startled Michael so, that he ran as quick as a rabbit and jumped right back into bed. "I'll try again tomorrow," he said to himself as he snuggled under the covers. "I better sleep while it's quiet in here." He yawned and closed his eyes.

The next night, as usual, the baby cried
and in came Mommy to take the baby out.

Michael decided this time that he had better
move a little faster so, he hopped out of bed
and half walking, half running to the bedroom door.
He peeked out. "So far, so good," he thought.

All Michael could see was the empty hallway.
Mommy and the baby were probably in the living room.

Off he marched toward the living room,
when suddenly his father appeared.

"And where are you going, young man?" his father asked.
Michael was so startled, he couldn't open his mouth.
"Caught again," Michael said to himself.

Since Michael was only eighteen months old,
he couldn't talk very well yet.

He knew how to say"hello, juice, cookie, thank you,
please," and a few other words. But, he didn't know
how to tell his father that he wanted to find out
what happens to the baby when
Mommy takes her out of the bedroom every night.

All he could think
of saying was, "Juice please."

Michael's father took him into the
kitchen and gave him a glass of orange juice to drink.

Michael sipped his juice, looking around all the while —
he might see Mommy and the baby. But, he didn't.

"Baby cry," Michael said finally,
trying to make his father understand.

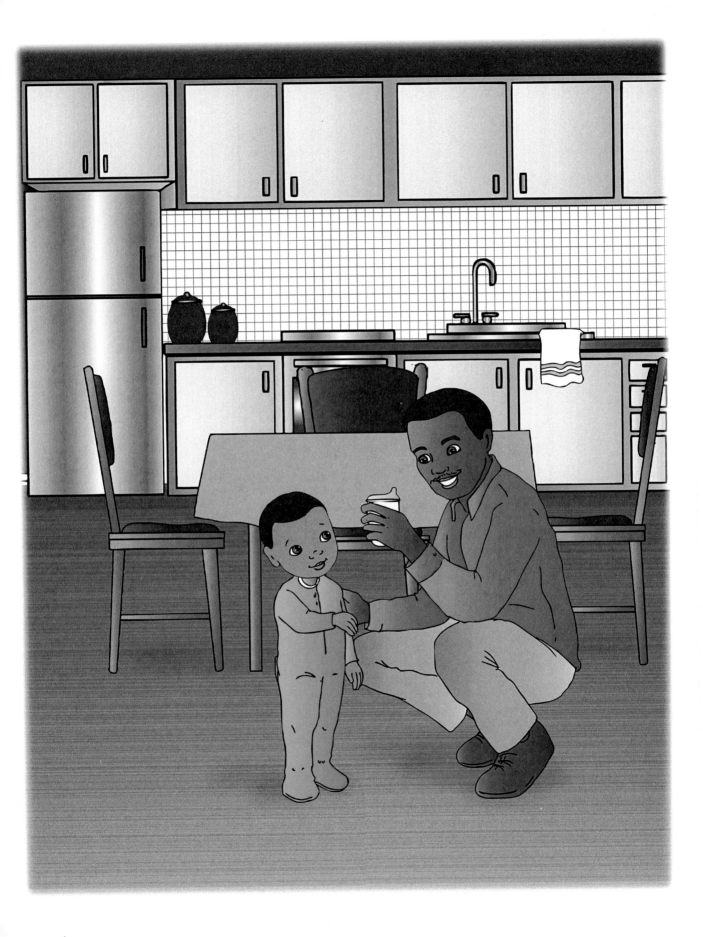

But his father only answered, "yes,"
and gently led Michael back to his room.

"I'll try again tomorrow," Michael sighed.

The next night, for some reason,
the baby went to sleep right away when Mommy
put her in the crib. Michael would just have to
wait until tomorrow.

Tomorrow came and it was bedtime.
The baby cried but Michael was soooo sleepy
that night, that he fell asleep before
Mommy came in.

It looked as if Michael would never
find out what happens to the baby.

Then the big night finally came.
As usual, the baby cried and cried.

Michael just listened and waited.
Mommy came in and took the baby out.

This time, Michael jumped out of bed
and ran as fast as his little legs could take
him into the living room.

And, there was Mommy, sitting on the sofa
with the baby on her lap.

The baby was drinking a bottle of milk.

Her eyes were half closed, and then all of a sudden,
she plopped her head back and fell fast asleep.

"Is that all?" thought Michael, "Just a bottle of milk
and poof! The baby is asleep? She didn't even finish it."

Michael was puzzled, "Maybe there's something special about this milk."

He walked over to the sofa, reached for the bottle and tasted the milk.

"This tastes like plain old milk!" Michael was disappointed.

"This is the same old milk she drinks all the time. She just had some at dinner and it didn't make her sleepy then!"

Mommy saw Michael drinking the milk and said, "Michael that's the baby's milk. Come, let's get both of you back to bed."

Michael followed his mother back to his room, climbed into bed and gave her another hug and kiss.

Michael looked at his sister asleep in her crib. He thought, "Babies are really dumber than I thought," and he was off to sleep too.

52363979R00015

Made in the USA
San Bernardino, CA
18 August 2017